SQUARING
THE
CIRCLE

SQUARING THE CIRCLE

A pseudotreatise of urbogony
FANTASTIC TALES

by Gheorghe Săsărman

A selection of tales
translated by Ursula K. Le Guin
from the Spanish translation by Mariano Martín Rodríguez

SEATTLE

Published by Aqueduct Press
PO Box 95787
Seattle, WA 98145-2787
www.aqueductpress.com

10 9 8 7 6 5 4 3 2 1

ISBN: 978-1-61976-025-7
Library of Congress Control Number: 2012953161

Cover painting: "The Tower of Babel, 1604" by Abel Grimmer

Book Design by Kathryn Wilham

Printed in the USA by Thomson-Shore, Inc.

Contents

Translator's Introduction:
The Road to π v

Author's Postscript to the
French edition of *Squaring the Circle* x

1. Vavylon... 1

2. Arapabad 5

4. Tropaeum 9

5. Senezia...15

8. Castrum 19

9. ... .23

11. Gnossos 29

13. Poseidonia..33

14. Musaeum 37

16. Kriegbourg 41

17. Moebia, or The Forbidden City 47

19. Arca 53

20. Cosmovia 55

21. Sah-Harah 59

24. Plutonia..67

25. Noctapiola..73

26. Utopia..77

27. Oldcastle..81

29. Dava..85

31. Hattushásh..93

32. Selenia...101

33. Antar...107

34. Atlantis...113

35. Quanta Ka...117

Translator Biography...122

Author Biography...124

Translator's Introduction:
The Road to π

A year or two ago I was sent a handsome little book titled *La Quadratura del Círcolo*. It was inscribed to me in English and a language that I thought was Romanian. With it was a charming letter from Mariano Martín Rodríguez, explaining that the book was his translation from the Romanian original by Gheorghe Săsărman, and that both he and the author hoped I would find it interesting and might have some idea how to go about finding someone to translate it into English.

The book was a set of brief stories, each about a different city—like Italo Calvino's *Invisible Cities*, of which I'm very fond. That similarity was interesting, and the first couple of stories seemed promising, but I was busy, and my Spanish is slow. So after thanking the sender and author I did nothing about the book for quite a while. But it kept on lying around in one place or another in my study. Maybe just because I liked the cover (a splendid Tower of Babel by an anonymous Fleming), or maybe because it was exerting the effect.

Some books, unread books, exert the effect. It's not rational, not easy to explain. They don't glow or vibrate, though that's what they'd do in an animated movie. They just are in view, they're there. There's this book, on the shelf in a book store or the library or like this one in a pile on my desk, and it is visible, silently saying *read me*. And even if I have no idea what it is and what it's about, I have to read it.

So, gradually, I obeyed. My motivation really wasn't all that irrational. Since I wasn't writing stories, I was looking for stories I might translate. I hadn't found anything in French. My Spanish (plus dictionaries) serves only for books written in a more or less "classic" vocabulary, which is why I could handle Mistral's poetry and Gorodischer's *Kalpa Imperial*, and these stories were definitely in that category. As I read more of them, the itch began to stir. Oh, hey, I wonder how this one would go in English…

I love translation, because I translate for love. I'm an amateur. I translate a text because I love it, or think I do, and love craves closer understanding. Translation for me is discovery, particularly in the two languages, Latin and Spanish, which I learned late and have no fluency in. I know I will not really comprehend a Spanish text until I have gone through the laborious and even humiliating process of trying to figure out how to express in English what it says and how it says it: a process of discovery.

This is equally true, in a way, of composing, writing my own work in my own language. I have always written to discover what to say and how to say it. But composition is a big undertaking, requiring great mental, emotional, and physical energy, which in my eighties I don't have. Translating, I have only to try to express the author's energy. I'm borrowing, stealing, imitating, using, living off of, colonizing, parasitizing, whatever you want to call it, the life-energy the author put into composition.

Also, translation is like revision. You fiddle and change and tweak and add and reduce and redo and ponder and look at the dictionary again and look at the thesaurus again and fiddle some more and listen until you get it as right as you can. I've always loved revising. It's part of the process of discovery—the easier part.

So I played with translating some of the Săsărman stories. Mariano sent me the Romanian original and Hélène Lenz's French translation, both of which were of use when my Spanish got stuck or I wanted to see the original wording (for Romanian is after all a Romance language, half-familiar even if unreadable to me). Meanwhile Mariano and I had begun to correspond by email. Everything went along very happily, as if it had been intended all along to happen. I couldn't find a translator because I didn't know anybody who knows Romanian, but I thought if I translated a few stories, maybe my agent could place them in a magazine. Meanwhile I thought about publishers who might consider a selection of the stories. Given its nature—fantastic, intellectual, ironic, experimental—the first publisher that came to mind was Aqueduct Press. I wrote Aqueduct and asked if they might be interested.

And well, so, here is the book.

You see why I take it seriously when a book does that *read me* thing to me? The book knows what it's doing. It's doing what all living things do: perpetuating itself, staying alive, possibly reproducing....

And you also know by now that this book is a translation of a translation. Obviously the ideal way for a Romanian book to find its way into English isn't via Spanish. On the other hand, it's better than a dead end. And it involved an extraordinarily happy process of collaboration. I sent my translations four or five at a time to Mariano (whose command of English is almost as great as his generosity), along with pleas for help, admissions of confusion, and questions about what he thought the author meant. He responded with corrections, suggestions, explanations, encouragements, and occasional confessions of having had trouble translating the very same sentence. I believe Mr Săsărman was called upon once or twice to give the final, genuinely authoritative word (is it an eagle or a vulture?) The process was genial, and the result immensely better than anything I could have done by myself—though my pride demands that I claim all mistakes and misunderstandings as my very own.

There are 36 stories in the original: here are 24. Those I did not translate resisted my understanding in a fundamental way, or, in a few, I resisted identifying myself with the conventional attitude of a mid-20th-century European man towards women, curiously at odds with the urbane, humane, subversive, desperately ironic sensibility of the stories as a whole.

Mr Săsărman is only too used to seeing chopped-up bits and pieces of his book rather than the whole thing. Below is the note he wrote for the French edition, telling us of the coincidence of its having been written at the same time as the Calvino book that it is so like and so unlike, and briefly outlining the book's troubled career in its very troubled country of origin.

Perhaps a professional translator working direct from the original language will eventually square the whole circle for us in America. Until then, here is two-thirds of it—along with all the author's elegant and enigmatic illustrations, to focus the mind's eye on some of the unexpected sites that lie along the infinite road to π.

—Ursula K. Le Guin, June 2012

Author's Postscript to the
French Edition of *Squaring the Circle*

The idea of writing a book of brief descriptions of imaginary cities, condensing into it the grandeur and tragedy of five millennia of urban history, came to me by chance, while I was in charge of the Architecture and Urbanism section of the review *Scânteia*. A writer had protested in an open letter against the demolition of an historic building, and the editors asked me to respond, which I did by writing the story "Musaeum." It was the autumn of 1969, a year after the Russian tanks invaded Prague, an invasion openly condemned by Ceaușescu, a time when many people, not only in Bucharest, believed (what a mistake!) that Romania was evolving towards democracy.

The Romanian "cultural revolution" began in July of 1971, just as I was finishing the manuscript of the book. While writing I had given no thought at all to censorship, and was ingenuous enough to believe that my ironic or sarcastic comments on various types of urban civilization, and thus implicitly on certain social models, gave no grounds for interpretation as criticisms of the regime in power. I was quite wrong. Editors flatly rejected the manuscript, or asked me to make radical changes or add optimistic stories describing the *radiant cities* of Socialist Romania and the Communist citadels of the shining *golden future of humanity*. After four years of wandering, the book was published in 1975, without its geometrical illustrations, and mutilated by censorship; ten stories had been eliminated, and others showed the scars of the censor's scissors.

In 1979, Italo Calvino's *Invisible Cities* came out in Romanian translation in Bucharest. When I saw the date of its original edition, 1972, I realized that the two books, so alike in their peculiar character and so different stylistically, had been conceived and written at the same time. A strange coincidence! And I rejoiced in it, like a Sicilian discovering that he has a rich cousin in America.

Stories from *Squaring the Circle* appeared in periodicals or anthologies in Romania, France, Germany, Italy, Belgium, and Hungary, some even before the first publication of the book. The French edition was the first complete translation and, at the same time, the first publication of the complete book—twenty years after I finished writing it.

—Gheorghe Săsărman, July 1992

(The French translation by Hélène Lenz was published by Noel Blandin, Paris, 1992. Editura Dacia, Cluj-Napoca, published the first complete Romanian edition in 2001. The complete Spanish translation is by Mariano Martín Rodríguez, Colmenar Viejo, La biblioteca del laberinto, 2010.)

1.

Vavylon

From a distance the city appears to be a ziggurat, but its interior layout is that of a beehive or termite mound on a colossal scale. In other words, far from being a solid tower of sundried brick, Vavylon is a series of vaulted levels, one above the other, containing tens of thousands of dark little rooms that once held the entire population of a city.

A brief but striking reference to it may be found in John 10:5: Babylon the Great, the mother of harlots and abominations of the earth.

The name, particularly its meaning, remains a mystery. Some insist that it derives from vav-ili—ili signifying "ruler," or "realm," or "to rule." The problem is vav, a root not mentioned in any comparative study of Indo-European languages, but which might be derived from bab, "door." I myself am tempted to read this obscure word as "equality" or "freedom." Thus Vavylon could be translated as "realm of equality, of freedom," or as "the freedom to rule."

To return to my description: the city consisted of seven stories, each in a different color of brick. The sides of each story were shorter than those of the one beneath, so that the shape of the whole was a stepped pyramid. In the lowest, largest layer, colored dull white, the slaves lived and had easy access to the surrounding fields, which it was their job to cultivate. The second level, black, was assigned for a moderate rent to craftsmen and merchants, considered to be free men. The third floor was purple and was occupied by the army. The fourth, of blue brick, had belonged since the foundation of the city to the priests. Men of high rank lived on the fifth floor, colored orange. On the sixth, silver-plated level dwelt the king, the owner of the entire city. Rumor had it that fabulous treasures and works of art had long lain stored in rooms of the sixth floor, but nobody could claim to have actually seen them. And finally, the seventh story was the solid gold temple of the god Kaduk.

Ramps, very steep, very highly polished, led from story to story. Every morning servants specially trained for the task poured wineskins full of oil over them to keep them as slippery as possible. Descent from level to level therefore was rapid, and anybody could do it, whereas attempts to ascend were rarely successful, achieved only by the cleverest, most experienced climbers. All the same, the law declared all the inhabitants of the city equal and forbade ascent to no one. Consequently every evening, when the oil was drying out, a silent crowd gathered at the foot of each ramp—a great many people on the lower levels, not so many on the higher floors. Few had never tested their luck; still fewer had succeeded. And since the steepness of the ramp increased with each level, only a very few in all the long history of Vavylon had been able to go more than a level or two higher.

Before it could be put on view to visitors Vavylon had to pass seven times through fire and sword, be torn down and rebuilt, deserted and repeopled again and again. The Assyrians, the Elamites, the Hittites, the Persians, the Greeks, and the Arabs all had to crush it, like a series of steamrollers, so that, at long last, leveled, buried under the sands of the desert, it might be unearthed by archeologists and become an important tourist site.

But in the days of old, every night the high god in person would symbolically reaffirm the principle, upheld by law, of the equality of all the citizens. The astonishing gesture was made in this way: each evening the god chose a virgin from the slaves of the lowest level, married her, and enjoyed himself with her all night among games and festivals. At dawn, when the king (wearing special sandals that kept him from slipping) mounted the ramp to worship in the golden temple, he would find the slave girl's body on the golden bed, still warm; and he would hurl it down from that tremendous height, without the formality of a death certificate, or even a request for an autopsy. No girl ever survived the fiery embrace that assured her equality with immortal Kaduk. And if, sixteen centuries later, one of the four wives of the vizier of Samarkand had not given birth to Sheherazade, nobody would ever have dreamed that the tale of the god's nightly marriage might be pure hokum.

2.
Arapabad

They drew rein, dismounted, and amidst the welcoming salaams of faithful servants, withdrew to the shade of the arcades to refresh their sunburnt faces. They allowed themselves to be bathed and anointed with scented oils, they feasted, they indulged their ears with the threnody of flute and tambourine and their eyes with the swaying of virginal arms and bodies. They made love with their favorite wives, slept dreamlessly, and at dawn went down to the inner courtyards to compose meditative verses about the dew on the just-budding roses.

They had ridden far and wide across the earth, had known all the beliefs, all the cities of the world. The narrow, twisting alleys, blind walls, and crumbling minarets of their city no longer satisfied them. Not even the site it was built on suited them now. As for the languorous life behind those iron-barred doors, for which they had sighed during their wanderings, it now bored them unspeakably. So they gathered in the forecourt of the mosque and, while washing their feet with the purifying water, decided to burn the Koran, set fire to the city, and build another, a city without history and without peer. That very day they loaded their belongings and harems onto camels and demolished the buildings, leaving them in flames. They mounted their swift steeds and, followed by the slow millipede of the caravan, set off to find the perfect site for the incomparable city.

They wandered on for a long time without deciding to settle down, for there was always some cause for dissatisfaction. And as time went by, doubt crept into their hearts. Were they in fact capable of doing what they had set out to do? Even if they found the ideal site, might not the city they built there have some accidental resemblance to the one they had destroyed, or to some other city? Some complained that the matter had not been talked over enough before they set off into the desert and thus provoked endless, useless arguments. The best minds among them fell to wondering if in fact their descendants would want to live in a city without a past, or if perhaps, following the example set them, they might burn it down and go off to found another. Such dire presentiments of calamity soon paralyzed all their initiative.

Ever since, that heretical people has wandered aimlessly across the sands. From time to time, as if to remind them of the curse upon them, there appears on the horizon the alluring mirage of the city never built. And for a little while they are all possessed by a frantic and delusive joy.

4.
Tropaeum

In the beginning was the jungle. Deep within it, far from the boggy margins of the river, in a clearing surrounded by high palisades of reeds, a few huts sheltered a tribe of gatherers, hunters, and fishers. Several times a year hurricanes swept over the vast green expanse leaving devastation behind, but always, around uprooted tree trunks and among lightning-charred stumps, the forest rose up again, even more suffocating and tyrannical. The tribespeople, used to repairing their huts rapidly and easily, now and then accompanied the rebuilding with a rite, which then was passed on down to their descendants, with amplifications.

Tens of thousands of years passed before the people, while pushing back the jungle little by little towards the south, began to domesticate cattle and moved out into the wild pastures of the lowlands. Now, when hurricanes laid the village waste, they built larger, solider houses, using tree trunks torn by the river from its banks. As time went on, timber began to grow scarce.

After a few millennia, a great forest fire reduced the entire settlement to ashes, destroyed the herds, and burned the pastures. The one-time herdsmen moved down closer to the river, improvised shelters of adobe and, in the course of learning how to scatter the good seed in the fertile mud left by spring floods, became farmers. And as they had begun to believe in gods and continued to fear fires, they sent their old people to negotiate tribal arrangements with the gods by burning them alive.

More centuries passed. Floods on the river obliged them to build dikes, to dig drainage ditches, and to relocate the city at a higher elevation. They discovered how to bake brick and built city walls, towers, gateways; they constructed ships and a port. As merchants, they worked their way down to the mouth of the river. About that time various epidemics broke out among them, worst of all the plague. The few survivors threw their dead onto bonfires as canny offerings to the bloodthirsty gods and set out to do everything all over again.

Some more decades went by. The capricious river changed course, leaving the city high and dry, deprived of the benefits of commerce. Fortunately an enterprising king ordered the digging of a navigable canal, enlarged the old port, and established another on the new waterway. He founded a dynasty, made advantageous alliances, arranged several marriages, and sent galleys all over the Mediterranean.

But not many years after his death a fearful earthquake left the city in ruins. Still the people did not accept defeat. The king's worthy successor rebuilt everything in stone and raised marble altars, on which hundreds of prisoners were sacrificed by cutting out their hearts in an effort to appease the undying anger of the gods.

An abrupt change of climate followed the earthquake. The whole region baked into a desert under the torrid heat of the sun. Before many months had passed, the specter of famine stalked the streets. The visionary architect-king was assassinated and replaced by a triumvirate, who soon succeeded in establishing huge works of irrigation. With the sea-port thriving as never before, the city established her first colonies on neighboring coasts.

Within a few weeks, a volcanic eruption buried the city under a thick layer of ash. The citizens, having fled the danger zone at the outset, cleared the ash from their houses in record time and repaired damages with remarkable resolution and diligence. The colossal bronze statue of their high god was heated red hot and stuffed full of orphaned children.

Once again, it appeared that the sacrifices were made in vain. After a few days, the entrance to the port was found to be blocked by an immense sand bar. Many ships ran aground on it, and the harbor was soon irrevocably choked with sand. Never had the threat of ruin hung so heavy. The triumvirate dissolved itself. A dictator crushed a disorganized effort at resistance by a coup d'etat. He constructed an ingenious network of causeways, replaced the lost port with seven new ones, and conquered the southwestern portion of the Mediterranean basin, establishing a true empire of the sea.

The empire existed only briefly. With no declaration of war, the cohorts of far-sighted Rome invaded in one merciless onslaught. In only a few hours, the capital city, so often restored to an ever more turbulent life after its confrontations with implacable Nature, was leveled to the ground forever. War accomplished what an endless history of adversity could not. Once the entire population had been sacrificed to the Latin gods and plowed under deep furrows on the site of the redoubtable citadel, the Romans celebrated their absolute and supremely efficient victory by raising a monument.

It lasted for a few minutes.

From that moment, calamities, cataclysms, and catastrophes of Nature spread in every direction from the site of Tropaeum throughout the world, leaving in their wake despair, the lust for glory, and the fearful, irreversible rivalry of neighbor with neighbor.

5.
Senezia

Once farmers lived here. Once, where the ruins are now, there were fertile fields, and a few huts sheltered the humble possessions of a hard-working people. But that was a long time ago, so long ago that even archeologists aren't certain about it.

Next came generations of stonecutters and carpenters, architects and sculptors. They established the most enchanting city known to history. They built palaces and cathedrals, laid out boulevards and forums, dug canals and wells; they peopled squares, bridges, and parks with fantastic statues of bronze and marble, and adorned the walls of buildings with frescoes and inlaid designs, the vaults with gold mosaic, the windows with stained glass. The early kings, warlike and covetous, outdid the greatest cities of the continent in power and arrogance, pillaging them for gold, silver, pearls, and gems. Later, wiser kings gathered treasures of art, precious books and manuscripts, thus adding to supremacy in wealth the superlative of learning and refinement.

Soon all the world came to know the glory of Senezia. As generations passed, the peerless city became a gathering-place of the elite; here royalty and dignitaries sent their offspring to study, here the young nobleman or gentleman spent his honeymoon, here the millionaire came to look for entertainment, the old maid to seek her last chance, the dowry-hunter to find his victim, the famous author to work on his new *roman-fleuve*. And since talk of money was considered ill-bred, they all worked hard at displaying their subtle understanding of Senezian architecture, art, and literature. The people of the city did well out of the tourists, to the point where tourism became their only source of income.

Proud of their remote forebears, but indulging their own inferiority complex and their profound distaste for work, the citizens abandoned their city to the caprices of Time. And Time did its duty. Walls gave way under the pressure of vaulted ceilings, foundations crumbled under the weight of walls, columns cracked, beams broke, domes collapsed. Rubbish buried the statues, weeds invaded the parks, trash fouled the forums and choked the canals. With ready benevolence, the world's museums made offers for whatever could be saved from imminent disaster.

The descendants of the haughty founders of Senezia resorted to theft and beggary. Visitors, ever fewer but still drawn by the grandeur of the ruined palaces and the legends of the place, soon were obliged to hire actual armed guards to escort them. Gaunt, ragged, and disdainful, the inhabitants received their wealthy guests with outstretched palms. With equal disdain, with a sneering envy, the visitors dropped a copper or two into the filthy hands.

After endless procedural debates and the failure of many resolutions to win the necessary majority, the prestigious Commission for the Protection of Monuments, an arm of the World Confederation of Nations, voted to allot a modest sum to finance the dubious project of salvaging what little might yet be saved. But the plan was never carried out, foiled by the resolute opposition of the Senezians, who in a final, startling outbreak of ancestral pride, refused all assistance.

Abandoned, forgotten, suffocated by the rapacious growth of weeds, the pompous ruins wait deep in the jungle for the learned archeologists of future times, while the last descendants of the Senezian race, organized into a secret cult, go about the world prophesying its imminent destruction.

8.
Castrum

Before the Twelfth Legion, the Orthogonic, occupied the region, nothing was there but a dusty road snaking along between wooded hills to avoid meeting the capricious river. The bogs sprayed mosquitos every summer at hurrying troops of travelers. The woods were full of game, echoing with the chatter and trill of birds. The city had not yet been born.

They started by replacing the road with a straight highway, stone-paved, provided with viaducts and bridges, direct as a saber-stroke.

They imprisoned the river at its source and elevated it into an aqueduct carried on a row of obsessively equal arches standing on thousands of granite pylons. They used the empty riverbed for stones and gravel.

Centuries-old trees became stacks of planks and beams; the roots were torn out and burned.

The bogs dried up. The peat was used to fire stupendous brickworks. They made millions of bricks, floor tiles, ceramic pipes to drain and transport water.

On the slopes of the nearby hills they dug quarries from which they cut great, regular blocks of limestone.

They leveled hills, filled up valleys and lowlands. They tamped down an immense square platform, its sides aligned by the compass.

Still the city had not been born.

They dug a double line of ditches and raised earthworks on the four sides of the platform. Within these they built a high, solid wall with massive towers at each corner.

Yet still the city had not been born.

The commander of the legion summoned his four immediate subordinate officers, and, sketching a square in the dust with his swordpoint, divided it with two strokes into quarters.

"Understood," his officers said, concisely, and returned to their sub-legions.

Next day they marked out on the platform the two principal streets, the *cardo* and the *decumanum*. At their crossing was the Forum, and at the end of each was a fortified gate with a drawbridge. Once the commander had taken up residence in the Forum, his four chief officers summoned their immediate subordinate officers, and each, sketching a square in the dust with his swordpoint, divided it with two strokes into quarters.

"Understood," their subordinate officers said, concisely, and returned to their sub-sub-legions.

During the following days, in each quarter of the platform two streets at right angles were marked out, and the officers took up residence at the crossing, where they then summoned their subordinate officers and showed them how to divide a square into quarters. This operation was repeated square by square and street by street in decreasing order of rank until the whole platform had been divided into little squares, down to the lowest ranks, who had no subordinates. In the center of each square where the two alleys crossed, the soldiers built identical houses, square, sturdy, each with a courtyard and a cistern.

Now the city was ready. Every street and alley crossed at right angles. The layout neatly reflected the hierarchic structure of the legion, prevented superior officers from getting lost, and rendered evasion of duty by the lower ranks all but impossible. The chain of command was superb. Orders were transmitted with prodigious speed. The city functioned perfectly. But one day the barbarians attacked.

At a high cost in casualties they forced one of the supposedly impregnable gates and burst into the city. Ignoring the streets, in which the defenders displayed impeccable defensive strategies, the barbarians attacked everything from all sides at once, even trampling the shoots just sprouting in the anguished soldiers' vegetable plots. They set fire to the houses, slaughtered men who hadn't expected to be attacked in their kitchen gardens, and broke into the Forum. In this moment of utter undoing, a lance struck the commander of the legion in the head, bursting open his skull. His subordinate officers beheld, horrified, a square brain deeply marked with a regular pattern of right angles.

Overwhelmed by panic and despair, the legionaries threw down their arms.

In times to come, the historians of Rome would ascribe this defeat to the barbarians' ignorance of geometry.

9.
...

We don't know its name, nor even if it had a name—yet another justification of its reputation as the world's most controversial city. At times even its existence has been questioned, perhaps rightly so, since so far we have found only four documents testifying to it, and each one to some extent contradicts the others. Here they are, abridged:

Our mission had been accomplished. [...] The Great Wall of China would look like an anemic worm compared to the gigantic city we have built, its robust body extending without interruption, just as we planned, from the Atlantic to the Pacific, a monumental esplanade some 4000 kilometers long, crossing the perilous jungles of the Amazon and the great chain of the Andes like a rainbow of peace arching over the body of America. [...] My memory was still crowded with images of our work: the heavy trucks bringing prefabricated buildings and carrying off huge trees torn up roots and all from the jungle as we advanced; bulldozers, cranes, steamrollers, the whole army of metal monsters whose racket my ears had been accustomed to for years and years; my teammates' fever-ravaged faces; the frowning gaze of the section chiefs at every new obstacle on our path…

All that was left far behind when we reached the west coast. Only a day had passed since that momentous event. My companions were asleep, stretched out on the warm sand, rocked by the sound of the breakers they had dreamed so long of hearing. They had earned their rest. Under the healing caress of the evening breeze, I abandoned myself to drowsiness.

I have no idea how many hours, or perhaps days, I lay there as if overcome by a sleeping-spell. When we woke, the city, all those last buildings we had admired from the beach before we slept, had vanished. No one has seen it since, and all my efforts to penetrate the mystery have been in vain.

(From the diary found among the possessions of the celebrated explorer Félix Fortuneau, who disappeared in the Mato Grosso in 1928.)

▲
▲▲

We are informed by reliable sources that after three weeks of negotiations, the employees of Nature and Landscape Safeguard Co. have won a 2.7% pay raise; it is expected that work will resume tomorrow. […] The strike was caused by discontent caused by certain unclear clauses in the contract.

> It would seem that the Company is attempting
> to remove the buildings of a city the name of
> which it has not so far revealed (but which is
> uninhabited, according to our informants) and

to restore the original, natural surroundings by means of massive replanting. The workmen's contract commits them to remain in the employ of the Company until the work is completed […] also including the possibility that this may take some time. Although the city does not appear to be more than seven kilometers long, after eight years of systematic anticlimax the workmen are still on the job. Rumor has it, moreover, that their distance from the far edge of the city remains, roughly speaking, constant. (From *Prensa* News Agency, informational bulletin No. 13,768, 8 September 1975, folio 16.)

▲
▲▲

My clearest memory of the city I finally discovered, with so much effort, in the very heart of the forest, 500 miles west of where I had expected to find it, is a conversation I had with a driver. […] I was about to leave when I saw him pull off to the right and climb down from the high cabin of his vehicle. He was sweaty and his overalls were smeared with oil; I thought he was after a pack of cigarettes or, like so many of them, some cold pineapple juice, and since I'd just been thinking of asking how I might get to Porto Velho and was glad to see somebody turn up so promptly, I went back into the bar and perched on one of the high stools, acting casual but keeping an eye on him as he came in the door and up to the bar. He took the seat next to mine, and for a while neither of us said anything, sipping our drinks and checking each other out.

"Might be a good idea to clear out," he said suddenly, not looking at me. "What the hell are you doing here anyway?— You think nobody noticed you?" he added, as I kept silent. He turned, bar-stool and all, toward me.

"Anything against it?"

"Listen to what I tell you and quit showing off. Some funny stuff goes on here. There's been others here, better men than you, all of them left, and good riddance. […] You know what I've been doing for four years? I drive that damn wreck all day back and forth across the city, on the main road. Going I carry prefabs, coming back I carry trees."

"Why do you stay?"

"We're stuck here. All of us here. We've got a contract… If it wasn't for the money I'd have cleared out long ago. The guy paying us must be crazy. If he does pay us…"

"If?"

"We don't get a cent till we finish the job."

He got up then as if he'd remembered something important and went straight out without another word and without paying. I told the waiter to put my strange buddy's drink on my bill.

"The gentleman has an account with us," the waiter explained with a politeness under which I sensed a knowing, disdainful smirk.

(From O. Nyr-Desseus, *In Search of the Ends of the Earth*, Paris, Editions de l'Equateur, 1977, pp 271-273.)

▲
▲▲

To all appearances, the city was perfectly axial, its length approximately 6.7 km, with a constant width of 530 m. What distinguished it from all other terrestrial cities, at least from the image received at the height of our station, was the truly amazing fact of its extremely slow movement from ENE to WSW, the velocity varying between 30 and 52 m/h. While in motion, its shape throbbed almost imperceptibly. It was the unpredictability of these dilations and contractions that reduced us to giving its length only as an average. During the nearly six years we spent in observing it, it traveled over 2000 km, from the center of the continent to the Peruvian coast, where it appears to have submerged gradually into the Pacific Ocean.

(From the lecture "Elements of Experimental Urban Cosmology," presented 24 April 1980 before the Académie française by a group of observers from Orbital Station KL-9.)

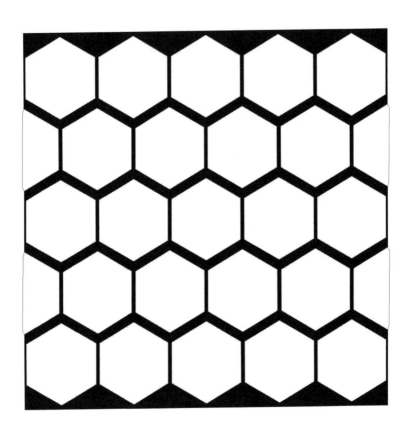

11.
Gnossos

Drunk with happiness, Icarus let the wind fill his wings like the swelling sails of a ship. He was flying now at such a dizzy height above the Labyrinth that it looked like a mere toy. And that was the enormous palace they had worked so hard, for so many weeks, to build!

He heard Dedalus calling him, urging him to hurry onward lest their escape be discovered while King Minos' famous fleet might still retake them.

At that moment, as if a light shone out in his mind, he understood that he could not leave this place. There was only one way to escape, and it was pointless to seek it anywhere else. The experience of flying had driven out all fear, and he no longer shared his father's impatience. He began to circle majestically, serene as an eagle after a successful hunt. The updraft bore him ever closer to the Sun.

"Fly lower!" Dedalus called to him. "The wax in your wings will melt!"

Icarus kept soaring in great spirals, higher and higher. Now he could see the whole island in one glance.

"Stop that foolish game!" shouted Dedalus in exasperation.

But, needing to save his strength for the long flight to Sicily, the architect father had fallen far behind and could no longer make himself heard. Icarus waved a hand to him in farewell.

Now the minuscule, white-walled structure beneath him occupied all his attention. He hovered a moment, suspended in air, drops of melting wax tickling as they ran down his back. Then, freed from the obsession of escape, he let himself drop downward like a shooting star. His vertiginous fall described an ever-decreasing spiral, while in his fascinated gaze the Labyrinth grew ever larger.

His all-seeing eyes no longer recognized the palace. Its whole plan, which he knew so well that he could have drawn it with his eyes closed, was utterly transformed. Not a trace of the maze remained, not one of the tortuous, deceptive corridors leading nowhere. The Labyrinth now appeared like an immense beehive whose innumerable curiously shaped, high-walled rooms offered no possibility at all of communication amongst them.

The cells of this gigantic honeycomb kept growing more numerous, and also, with fearful speed, growing clearer, Icarus could distinguish the smallest details. At the same time, the honeycomb itself was enlarging, increasing, spreading out clear to the horizon. It was no longer a palace but a whole city. In almost every cell, a person provided with a ball of yarn was trying to find the way out, evidently not suspecting that even if he succeeded in getting through the wall he would only find himself in another cell where his search would have to begin all over again. But not even so illusory an escape was permitted to the wretched captives. The entire universe in the center of which each one found himself consisted of insurmountable, impenetrable, blindingly white walls, and a useless ball of yarn.

Each of them had ended up there by his own choice. Where was the invisible Minotaur each one had imagined he was going to slay with the sword at his hip?

Icarus descended rapidly, unseen, over the heads deep in thought. The trajectory he had traced through the air ended on the marble flagstones of a vacant cell. The silent existence of the hive-city pursued its course as if nothing had happened.

Mastering his grief, Dedalus winged his weary way towards the court of King Cocalus.

Yet unseen by any mortal eye, the red thread that slipped between Icarus' clenched teeth had sketched on the white of the marble floor the intolerable solution, the only possible way out.

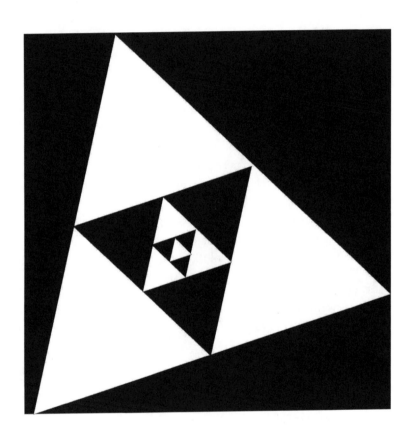

13.
Poseidonia

People will, in time, get used to living underwater. They will succumb to the temptation of the submarine palaces that stand at the moment empty, with their coral walls, their chandeliers of living pearl; they will be lured into the city's meandering streets, never sultry or freezing, never windy or rain-swept, and the bluegreen plazas lit by a soft, filtered sunlight, and the watery depths that know no fear of floods.

In time, their lungs will be familiar with the art of extracting oxygen from water, their taste-buds with the delicate flavor of algae and raw fish killed as they are eaten, their bodies with the skill of floating elegantly, undulating dreamily, and propelling forward like lightning. Their torsos will grow streamlined and their limbs adapted to swimming; their intelligence will grow sharper along with their noses. They will populate Poseidonia, living the good life in the abundance of the great aquatic plains. They will know the ineffable delight of the amphibious somersault, and will be less and less prone to nostalgia for the original, terrestrial, bipedal human condition.

In time, and increasingly, people will come to look like dolphins.

But until that time, oh, how hard it is to take the first step, learn the first rule, the golden rule of keeping up appearances: silence!

14.
Musaeum

It was a quite commonplace city, to begin with. Then by the decree of capricious Fate an unusual child was born in one of its commonplace houses. Refusing from his earliest years to accept the commonplace existence to which his parents tried with the utmost care and devotion to confine him, he took it into his head to storm the ineffable gates of immortality. Posterity recognized his genius—perhaps rather too promptly—and his example soon proved contagious. Which explains the fact that within a short time the city was bursting with geniuses, and there was scarcely a house in which one of the many personalities crowned by the glory of talent had not been born, or anyhow lived if only for a month or so.

And now, in an exhibition of amazing prophetic powers, the administration changed the city's name, calling it Musaeum, and adopted the famous Decision, from which a new era came to be dated. Even now the Musaeumians count the years from that day. A decree of profound wisdom, full of pious respect for history and the illustrious figures of their predecessors, the Decision prohibited with categorical ferocity the destruction of any house for any reason, on pain of death. Not a brick could be moved out of place; the slightest modification, exterior or interior, bore the risk of an unwelcome appointment with the firing squad.

Perhaps the Decision would not have endured in force so long—the city could not keep indefinitely extending outward—if one of the greatest inventors of all time (who, as might be expected, lived there) had not imagined a highly ingenious system enabling each new generation to erect new dwellings on the roofs of the old. Dozens of dead cities came to lie buried under the living city superimposed high above them.

An unusual division of labor came, in time, to limit the basic professions to three. The bulk of the population were employed in activities relating to the underlying cities: keeping a careful registry of the archives, they maintained detailed biographical notes on every single inhabitant of the city at every point in time, compiled voluminous treatises on the general history of the people, detailing every aspect of their social life, and investigated the architectural relationships of the various urban layers, the succession of styles, and their reciprocal influences with the rest of the world.

Those who practiced the second major profession of the Musaeumians were dedicated to the difficult operation of erecting the framework to support the city destined to house the next generation. A task clearly of the highest responsibility, demanding multilateral technical knowledge: a few young people distinguished in secondary school by diligence and professional integrity were annually initiated into its secrets.

The third profession, practiced by a very few, the rare elite, was the creation of immortal works celebrating the marvelous existence of the citizens of Musaeum. Now and then one of the creators went astray, permitting himself veiled allusions to what that existence might have been had the city never adopted the Decision; rightfully indignant, the people would stone him to death, since lynching was illegal.

The full list of dozens of generations of authentic creators occupied a special place in the historical treatises. Their houses were museified, and commemorative plaques marked every step of their passage through life. It is the unfortunate truth that their works remained completely unknown, since nobody took the time to look at them. Not even the other creators could perform this mutual service, being far too busy with their own creations.

Nights, when the tumult of the carpenters up on the rooftops ceased, the silence of the city was sometimes broken by a dull, nerve-wracking, droning sound arising from the very depths. Unnerved, the Musaeumians locked themselves into their houses and got drunk, or took sleeping pills, or stopped their ears to shut out the noise. A few brave citizens had now and then ventured down among the cities of the past, but not one had returned.

And no one knew if these nocturnal sounds were the groans of the immense framework bowing under the weight of all that lay above it, the whistle of the wind through ruins, the meaningless murmurs of the unburied victims of lapidation, or possibly the shrill chorus formed by the squeaking of millions of rats…

16.
Kriegbourg

"The devil with it," Richard said, shading his eyes with his hand. "It won't be easy to get a close look at these good folks' treasury."

Henry said nothing. He had taken in with one gaze the citadel's robust fortifications, crowned by the orange banner with a red lion embroidered in its center. He had assessed by eye the thickness of the walls, the depth of the moats, the strength of the gates; he had estimated the hidden danger of the battlements, ramparts, and machicolations; he had calculated the probable number of defenders, weighed the relative strengths of the two forces and the possibility of success in a siege.

"Just look at those towers!" Richard insisted. "More even than in Florence! Think of the gold, think of the jewels in the stinking vaults under the city hall!"

"Let it be," the Prince said, frowning.

"Think of the women languishing, the girls perishing of secret longings! We must not be selfish…"

Henry laughed aloud and, touched at his vulnerable point, shouted, "To horse!"

The blue flag with its roses flew out gallantly with the resounding gallop of the warhorses. Visors lowered, the knights stormed the nearest gate. Taken by surprise, the city's defenders had neglected to raise the drawbridge, and the sentinels were asleep at their posts. The assault was terrific. Before the pitch was heated, before the oil and water were boiling, before the guards had gathered, the attackers had taken the first bastion and cleared their way into the citadel. A hideous butchery took place within those walls. The defenders fought savagely, and not one let himself be taken alive. They gave way step by step, house by house, filling the narrow ways with corpses.

After five days and five nights of mayhem the last defender cut his own throat with his sword rather than surrender. By then the city was a sinister sight. Decomposing bodies lay everywhere, and the wind carried the foul odor into every corner.

The fearsome conquerors breached fat casks in the cellars of the finest houses and devoted themselves to swilling. Then, stinking of blood, sweat, and garlic, unshaven, emboldened by drink, they made their triumphal entry into the boudoirs of the weeping widows, tumbled them onto plump cushions and consoled them with great conviction. Many young women, after an unconvincing show of grief, appeared quite willing to be consoled, and maidens let themselves be persuaded with remarkable ease.

Then they all slept in a heap for a whole day.

"I believe you said something about treasure," the prince murmured. Richard groaned while putting on his shoes.

"Coffers full of riches, all locked away, waiting for us in the vaults under the city hall…"

On the way there, Henry felt a strange discomfort. He stared up at the blue banners they had raised on the turrets to replace the orange ones. He looked about. There seemed to be too many corpses, somehow. And some of them seemed too far decayed. His uneasiness grew when he saw several skeletons white with age lying in an alley. Unthinkable that the inhabitants of the place had left their dead unburied.

"What do you make of those bones?"

"Might have been there for months," said Richard.

"Or years," the prince muttered, pensive.

Oppressed by apprehension, Henry descended the stone steps. And indeed riches were there, brimming over from jewel-encrusted gold and silver vessels and chests full of doubloons, pearls, and precious stones. They forgot their worries for a while, feasting their gaze on the fabulous treasures, as the gold and diamonds flashed in the torchlight.

All at once the prince nudged Richard. All around the treasure lay dead bodies, dozens of corpses in various states of decomposition, with clothing, armor, and arms from every country in the world. At that moment he saw the truth with horrible clarity: he saw how warriors, drawn by the opulence of the citadel, had kept coming to attack it, wave after wave of them through the years, and how the besiegers, drunk with victory and worn out by orgies, would fall easy prey to the next siege... He shuddered with a presentiment of fast-approaching doom.

"Out of here!" he shouted, terrified.

"Out?" Richard turned on him. "Are you mad?"

"We've got to get out while there's still time! Look out!" The unfortunate prince was halfway up the steps before the other man drove his sword between his ribs.

Henry dropped back dying among the other bodies.

"There really was too much for two men," Richard remarked nostalgically.

A few hours later another set of brave knights assaulted the citadel, craving riches and sex, and bearing before them a purple flag embroidered with two golden snakes. They arrived in close ranks, powerful, implacable, ready to prove to Richard that what he had found in the gloomy vault was too much even for one man.

17.
Moebia, or The Forbidden City

He had read in the memoirs of Marco Polo that the famous capital was composed of concentric enclosures connected by monumental portals, over which tiled roofs towered one above the other, pagoda style. The first enclosure was the Outer City, then came the Mongolian or Middle City, and the Inner or Imperial City; and finally, in the center, was the Forbidden, the Sacred City. There no European had yet penetrated. The guide had warned him that he would fail in the attempt, but he never considered giving up, determined to be the first foreigner to enter the Sacred City.

"Very well," said the guide, "follow me."

They passed through the first circle without much trouble. The streets were straight, and the houses, as well as he could make out, followed the plan of the city on a reduced scale, in concentric rings. The inhabitants looked so much alike that he could tell them apart only by their clothing; they went about their business without taking any apparent notice of him. At the second portal, he was asked to show his papers. The Mongolian City was much the same as the Outer City, but its inhabitants paid even less attention to him. He had to wait a long time before he was permitted into the Imperial City, with its palaces and gardens, but at last he was told that the Great Khan himself would receive him.

The Great Khan welcomed him smilingly with the ceremony due the envoy of a great power. He was served a twelve-course dinner, prepared in accordance with the recipes of the finest chefs of the Empire, and accompanied by twelve different kinds of tea. Then came a pantomime show with masked actors in grotesque costumes, followed by a troupe of girls who performed a graceful dance to an exotic melody.

The foreigner felt that the moment to make his request had come.

"Of course, of course," said the Great Khan, watching the hypnotic movements of the dancers with his unchanging smile. "Our guest will not object if, on his way to the Sacred City, he has to pass through several doors."

"Not at all, I've already begun to get used to it."

"I thought that might be the case," said the Great Khan, smiling. "Our guest will not take it amiss if at each door he is asked a question, since only the chosen, praise be to God! may enter the Sacred City."

"Not at all."

"Nor will he find it unjust," the Great Khan continued, "to offer his head as security each time he answers."

The foreigner said nothing. His blood ran cold.

"Our guest may always change his plans." The potentate gazed at him, smiling.

The foreigner mastered his fear and said, "I accept the conditions."

The Great Khan took up a little stick and lightly tapped a bronze gong. Two soldiers armed with swords appeared at once and led the visitor to the series of doorways through which he was to pass. Thus formidably escorted he came to the doorway where his daunting test would begin. The portal, set in a wall of enameled tiles, was of white marble, crowned by triple pagoda-roofs, their gilt blazing bright in the sunshine. Wooden deer-heads lacquered red jutted out beneath them. The double doors of bronze were shut. On a mat before the doors an old man, grey-haired and sparsely bearded, dressed in white, sat waiting for them, smiling. He bore an astonishing resemblance to the Great Khan, and to the soldiers, and the guide, and indeed every man the visitor had seen so far here; but, tormented by thoughts of the question he must answer, he had stopped wondering at anything.

"How many doors must you pass through to reach the Sacred City?" the old man said.

The soldiers hefted their swords, ready to pull them from the sheaths.

"If I give the right answer," said the foreigner, thinking aloud, "that means there will be one less to pass through."

The bronze doors swung noiselessly open. He had guessed right.

His escorts followed him into a passage between walls swarming with dragons in bas-relief. The splendid colors of the tiles were delightful. The high walls continued on, sinuously curving, crowned every so often with identical towers. After an hour of walking, his interest in the dragons and the colors of the enamel had been stifled by the wearisome monotony. When he came once more to a doorway roofed with gilded tiles, guarded by an old man with a sparse beard, he was not surprised to see the same enigmatic smile, the same bronze doors. But the sage, this time, was dressed in purple. Except for this one detail, and his tiredness from the long walk, he could have thought he was still facing his first test.

"What brings you into my presence?" the sage inquired.

The soldiers moved slightly, and he heard the hiss of steel blades sliding out of bronze sheaths.

"The benevolence of the Great Khan," he said.

Once again the bronze doors silently opened. Once again he was walking, intimidated, between the enameled walls.

So he came to the third doorway, and to the fourth, and each time he found the right answer to the question asked him by the sage with the sparse beard. And so on till the tenth doorway. There, worn out with walking, when the armed and menacing soldiers brought him once again to the marble portal and an old man, dressed in black, posed the inevitable question, his head was spinning so that he did not even understand it. The soldiers unsheathed their swords.

"How many doors have you passed through?" the old man repeated, smiling.

The swords were raised slowly in the air, their edges glittering.

"I have passed through ten," he said quickly.

The bronze doors did not stir. The soldiers held their swords high overhead. The foreigner asked himself if he should have counted in the three doorways he had come through before he faced the Great Khan, and, hurried and pleading, cried, "Thirteen!"

The sage smiled, stroking his sparse beard. And as the swordblades shivered like descending lightning he said, "You passed through a door ten times, yes, but it was always the same door."

And he bent to lift the bloodstained head from the tiled floor and throw it onto the heap of skulls that the foreigner had failed to notice.

19.
Arca

20.
Cosmovia

They had believed for a long time that what they considered their city was at the center of the universe, and that the various celestial bodies around it moved in obedience to the commandments of Staris, Cosmovia's legendary founder. Then one day an agile intellect among them demonstrated that the stars did not move randomly, as it might appear, but in conformity with precise laws; he proved, moreover, that mass, distance, and velocity determined the reciprocal relationships of stars and planets, galaxies and nebulas, that there was no fixed point in the Cosmos, no center of the universe, and that these same laws ruled Cosmovia's incontrovertible motion through extragalactic space, determined by the relative position of the nearer galaxies.

With astronomy on a sure foundation, Cosmovian scientific understanding entered a phase of spectacular development; hardly a week passed without a major discovery, and every month saw new fields of study established. Soon their knowledge had grown enough to permit them to decipher documents in the City Archives, long ignored. This extremely laborious work, undertaken by chance and assigned to a group of illustrious savants, produced startling revelations. In the first place, they realized that their city was simply an enormous starship gone out of control, now wandering through the deeps of space. Then, that Staris had in fact existed: he had been the ship's first captain. And finally, material in the documents indicated that at some point the members of the expedition had been attacked by strangers arriving, somehow, from somewhere. The struggle had been long and hard, and there was no record of its final outcome. Such, roughly and in sum, were the conclusions that could be deduced from the entire archive, or what now remained of the archive. Of course a great deal might have been destroyed during the fighting, or in the long years, no one knew how many years, of total ignorance that had passed since.

When the commotion caused by these sensational revelations had calmed down, the Cosmovians could begin to consider their profound meaning. They had come into possession of a prehistory, or more exactly, a protohistory. Suddenly they must ask the most dramatic questions: Where had they come from, and how long must they continue their absurd journey? But the worst torment was the fundamental uncertainty, the impossibility of establishing whether they were heroic survivors or ruthless aggressors. Not the slightest description of the appearance of either had come down to them, so that either hypothesis was equally possible. And moreover, they could not categorically refuse the idea that they might be descended from both the victims and the conquerors.

Several generations lived in the shadow of this awful ambiguity. Yet in the end the inhabitants of Cosmovia, tired of wondering if the blood in their veins was heroic or damnable, agreed that by now it really didn't matter at all. They went on to decide that even the absence of a goal to their journey made no difference; and some of them, considering that absence perfectly natural, even proved its necessity.

21.
Sah-Harah

Lord Knowshire could scarcely contain his emotion. Before him, only a few miles away, gleaming bright in the sunlight, were the red walls of Sah-Harah. In that moment he forgot the tragic vicissitudes of his journey, forgot the unhappy fate of his companions and the faithlessness of his guides, forgot all but the marvelous sight that lay at last before his eyes. For years he had dreamed of it, repeating the passages from Abu-Abbas engraved in his memory and comparing the Coptic inscriptions of Abydos with the papyrus, two millennia older, discovered in the nameless tomb at Deir-el-Bahari and never fully understood till now. He had followed his destiny here. He allowed himself a moment to savor the long-sought triumph, for he had paid dearly for it. Then, hoisting onto his back the knapsack containing all that was left of the expedition supplies, he set off resolutely toward the gleaming granite walls that sent him from afar a final, irresistible challenge.

The circular shape of the city became ever more apparent as he came nearer. He visually estimated the diameter as not less than two miles. The city presented to the visitor a forbidding exterior wall sixty or seventy feet high of polished, perfectly fitted stone blocks, an even surface without hollows or projections. It appeared to be a single colossal building: a cylinder with a slightly rounded lid. As his lordship came close, that lid or cap was hidden by the loom of the wall.

He came right up to the wall and set his palm on the red, sun-heated stone. Then he set off along it, seeking an entrance. He judged that he had gone about a quarter of the circumference when at last he came on an opening, very high, very narrow—so narrow that only an unusually thin person could venture to enter it. There he halted, slipping his pack off, and considered what to do.

The entrance—he could not bring himself to call it a doorway—was appallingly plain. An opening. A dark crack in the lower third of the featureless wall. Nothing frightening, nothing intended to give warning or strike terror into one who sought entry, no trace of bolts, bars, sphinxes, or chimera. And yet standing outside this entrance the intrepid Lord Knowshire felt a most disagreeable sensation, a shudder that ran clear through his body, head to foot. But it was too late to turn back now. The moment's hesitation past, he stepped across the invisible threshold.

Though famous for his thinness, and still leaner now after the long days of trekking in the heat of the desert, even he could go forward only by sidling along, his chin tucked into his shoulder, dragging his pack behind him by the strap. Contrary to his expectations and the usual mythologies, he came to no trapdoors, no hidden devices set to destroy the wiliest and most cautious transgressor. Quite the opposite: the tight squeeze of the entrance soon opened out into a corridor, not very wide, to be sure, but easy enough to walk in. Light came from high up; the air was breathable; the floor lay on a scarcely perceptible rising grade; the walls were featureless; and the passage had a slight, constant curve to the left, a curve evidently following the shape of the outer wall.

After walking some hours his lordship realized that the corridor was not circular, for if it had been he would almost certainly have come back round to the entrance or a place he had already passed. The passageway led steadily onward, turning always very slightly to the left. Unmistakably, he was tracing a slow, gigantic spiral, the end of which he could not foresee, since he could not precisely determine the curvature, not knowing the thickness of the walls, and thus could not know if the spiral extended all the way to the center of the colossal edifice or would end before that. All he could do was go on, following the constant slight curve to the left.

Nightfall is very brief in that latitude. All light in the corridor came from the sky, so when his lordship found himself in gloom and shadow, he had just time to look at his watch and set down his pack before it grew pitch dark. For hours he had heard no sound but his own footsteps amplified by echo. Now he listened hard, but in vain; not the slightest sound came to his ears. In the changeless quiet of the night his breathing and the slow rhythm of his heartbeat were the only signs of life. He closed his eyes. The image of the corridor, rocking a little to the cadence of his steps, rose before him and would not leave him. Then, worn out by fatigue and the effort to keep calm, he fell into a deep, dreamless sleep.

The night passed without event. Yet for the first time since he set off on this expedition, he woke with a vivid sense of the relentless passage of time. Once again he went through the limited contents of his pack: binoculars, a map, a broken compass, a journal in which he had made no entries for a long time, a book from which he had never been parted, some cartridges for the revolver at his belt, a canteen half full of stale water, biscuits, chocolate, a few tins of meat, a knife…and that was all. The food could be made to last several days. The water, maybe three. Not a reassuring assessment.

He set off again. He had to go on. For a moment he thought he had started out in the wrong direction, but that was impossible; the passage led on, curving slightly to the left; everything was as it should be.

The problem with this easy walking was only now becoming clear. A day passed, two days; well before a week had passed he was suffering from hunger and above all from thirst. His steps were less steady, his vision dimmed. The slight curve of the corridor began to obsess him. He could not sleep. He walked on even at night. Despite that utter darkness, the image of the changeless passage ahead was so deeply printed on his retina that it never left him, and he followed it all night. He walked on, not stopping, no longer knowing night from day, not counting the days, his mind fixed on the corridor's end, persisting in envisioning the unforeseeable. He shuddered with rage, fearing that he had got turned round, knowing he would die of thirst long before he reached his goal, terrified at the thought that his legs would give out, that he would fall down and crawl a while and die before he ever came to the end of the horrible corridor…

He staggered, fell. His knees hurt very much. Only then did he realize he had been walking in complete darkness. He reached out toward the wall for support. His groping fingers touched bones: a skeleton He struggled to his feet. Must go on. He knew that if he stayed there to rest he would never get up again. He went on, more cautiously. After a while there was some light, and he saw other skeletons. In a moment of clear-mindedness he realized that the radius of the circle within which he moved had greatly decreased; the leftward curve of the corridor was much more marked. It could not be much farther to the center. He breathed with difficulty. His tongue was swollen, his belly cramped with hunger-pangs. He decided to get rid of the backpack he had carried so far, useless to him now. He took off his shoes, then his clothes, one by one. The sense of fatality, of the irreversible, that he had waked to that first morning now filled his whole being.

When he stepped out naked into the round central chamber of the Nummultian city Sah-Harah, Lord Knowshire was at the end of his strength. He leaned against the wall, and before letting himself slip slowly to the floor, managed to take one look clear around the room. What he saw would have awed anyone: twelve massive golden thrones set around the wall, in which sat twelve bejeweled ivory statues of Osiris. The alabaster wall was carved in bas-relief, a great frieze of scenes from the Book of the Dead, broken by panels of hieroglyphs. In the center of the chamber, among bronze tables set with bowls and baskets filled with honey, wheat, wine, and dates, stood a magnificent silver sarcophagus. The lid was propped open on two cedarwood poles. Next to it, on a chair that looked very simple amid the pomp of all the rest, some purple garments were laid.

Spellbound, his lordship stood up straight and walked forward as if floating on the air. He no longer felt pain, hunger, thirst, or was no longer aware of them. He had entirely forgotten what had brought him to this place. As if sleepwalking, he approached the sarcophagus and, paying no heed to the opulent feast laid out on the tables, looked inside to make sure the coffin was empty. He moved slowly, with calm, hieratic gestures, as if carrying out a sacred rite. He took up the purple robes and put them on. Then, with great care not to bring the lid down, he slipped into the sarcophagus and stretched himself out, smiling a little. His death was a slow, quiet crossing of the boundary between the two worlds, as if no boundary existed.

He was dead. The rotten cedar-wood props shattered, spraying a fine dust all around, and the heavy lid of the sarcophagus came down with a mighty crash. On its upper surface was the carven image of Lord Knowshire's face, transfigured by an ineffable smile. It had been waiting there four thousand years for this reunion.

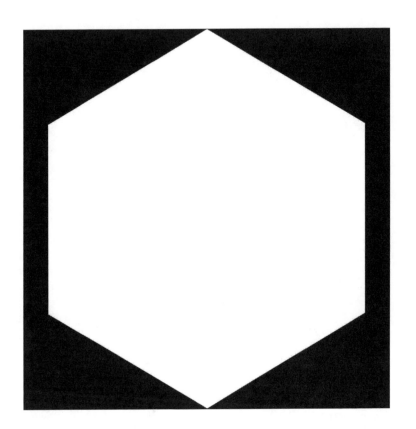

24.
Plutonia

He kept digging. For years, for centuries, ever since the creation of the world it seemed, he had been ceaselessly, tirelessly digging. He had by now completely forgotten what the initial impulse had been—the inevitability of a thermonuclear catastrophe, the overpopulation of the surface of the earth, some suddenly awakened ancestral instinct, or mere curiosity... In any case that initial impulse had lost all importance as he became convinced that the depths into which he endlessly tunneled were the only true world, and came more and more to see all supraterrene existence as deceptive, a sterile experience with no future, probably an illusion. He had never had any confidence in the surface cities, being deeply convinced that the ultimate essence of architecture lies in interior space. Up there in daylight, the exterior could never be wholly done away with. Here in Plutonia there was only the interior, the quintessence of true architecture. Here he had found his vocation.

The city now, for him, was a series of judiciously connected underground spaces—tunnels, corridors, rooms, shafts—whose shapes and dimensions were limited only by his imagination. A labyrinth he loved to run through, touching the smooth walls with his hands, ready to open a new working face wherever he found the rhythmic tension of the spatial flow unsatisfactory. It was indeed precisely this limitless possibility of transfiguration, this almost organic structural mobility, that he considered the greatest virtue of the subterranean city.

Digging satisfied him in every way: along with the ecstatic effort of planning each new trajectory, of integrating it all into one harmonious whole continuously envisioned anew, it gave him not only beneficent, healthful muscular labor, the rhythmic play of his body, but an overwhelming richness of being. His sight had grown weaker, to be sure, since he had to keep his eyes shut to prevent dirt from getting into them and was sometimes unable to open them at all; but then, what use were they to him? Perception of interior space was absolutely independent of visuality; it must be kept in mind that the Plutonian sense of interiority presupposed total darkness. And even if he could make a light, even if he could see, the resulting optical illusions would disturb his visual imagination. He could get on without seeing, particularly as it might distract him.

As for hearing, that was a different matter. His hearing had grown so sharp that he was quite sure he was the equal of any bat. By listening he could locate himself unerringly in the complex labyrinth of subterranean passages, recognize friends and enemies at a great distance, avoid crumbling or insecure rockfaces and corridors that threatened collapse. When he was working, he had only to stop digging for a moment to hear, in every direction, the sounds of intense activity. Digging was going on everywhere. Never, not for an instant, did he feel alone.

Nor was it a matter of hearing only, for his tactile sense was fully as acute. He was of course aware that his limbs had shortened, his hands and nails had enlarged; nearly blind as he was, he knew that, just as he knew that he had grown a complete coat of short, thick, fine fur. But with what precision, now, he could, purely by touch, even with the less sensitive parts of his body, distinguish strata of differing hardness or texture, tell the grain of gravels or sands, identify roots, foundations, pipes, pebbles! He recognized instantly, by feel, the botched job or the masterpiece of engineering. He felt that his own well-planned, ingenious vaults had been shaped for eternity.

But the most miraculous, the most powerful of his senses was doubtless the sense of smell. It enabled him to locate running water, springs, the water table, to keep well away from cemeteries, and to find food. Infallibly he scented out the larva's hiding place, the ants' nest, the soft thread of a young earthworm, the well-guarded hamster granary. Best of all, scent was his unerring guide to the maddening entwinements of love, the remembrance of which clouded his mind. He could imagine no more nearly perfect expression of bliss than the delirious pursuit by unforeseen routes through the colluding earth, and the culmination, a strange, explosive mixture of virgin timidities, perverse bites, the paradoxical embrace of two cylindrical, oily, dirt-encrusted bodies.

All the same, when, in his rare moments of rest, he let his mind wander, he did not think of past or future love-making, but inexplicably, significantly, of genesis. He imagined the

Great Builder, the supreme god of Plutonia, in the form of a giant mole, a demiurge digging the endless tunnels of the Universe through the musty shadows of nonexistence.

25.
Noctapiola

Seen from above, from high above, it looks like a great archipelago; closer up, like an immense forest, strewn with lakes. Only to the eyes of one walking through it does the city reveal its strange, aseptic character. Here as nowhere else on earth the embrace of earth and water, rocks and trees, the work of Nature and of Man, achieves a supreme harmony.

The houses, scattered seemingly at random around the lakes and ponds among pine and fir groves, stand quite far apart, and it would take a long time to visit them all. With their gleaming white window-sashes and picture windows admitting light all round, they provide an extraordinary degree of comfort; for example, every house enjoys the optimal temperature and humidity provided by a Swedish patent air-conditioning system.

The yellowish gravel of the winding paths is sorted, cleaned, and renewed every spring. On every lawn bronze and granite sculptures stand in a waking dream. Noctapiola is a city with no mud, no dust, no crime or theft or adultery. It is a city with no moon, hence no lovers. Life here might seem pretty boring.

And indeed nothing happens, during the day. The town looks abandoned. Among houses sunk deep in silence the deserted paths sketch vague question marks, as if to reinforce the mystery and melancholy of the statues. Hours pass unmarked; there are no clocks, the measurement of time is utterly forbidden.

When night falls (and the starless, moonless nights are long and dark) people begin to stir. Bright light suddenly illuminates rooms, and through the big windows people can be seen gathering around opulently laden banquet tables. Nobody has yet managed to explain how the world's finest delicacies arrive nightly to feed the Noctapiolans, just as nobody has provided a remotely plausible explanation of the purpose of the paths and the statues, since it is well known that the inhabitants of this Northern city leave their houses only one day in the year.

At midnight the lights go out. Take great care, foreigner, not to be caught after midnight in Noctapiola! Not one of the bold souls who risked the experience escaped with their life. At daybreak their mutilated, dismembered bodies were in no condition to tell what happened.

Once a year only, and only by special permission previously obtained, are foreigners allowed here past midnight: on the summer solstice. Nobody dies, that night. The sun itself hangs blood-red and motionless on the horizon, keeping darkness away. The few travelers who have taken the chance of being admitted to the city on this one white night tell, fascinated, how from the depths of the lakes rises a soft, nostalgic singing of inhuman voices. With that sound, hidden doors open and the Noctapiolans, haloed with refulgent light, come out and walk down the stone steps straight into the water. Young and old, boys and girls, women, children, as if in a drugged trance, they pace slowly down the damp steps and sink straight into the green, cold depths. Their bodies, marble-white and of pagan beauty, give themselves up naked to the waves, while the invisible voices die away. From the half-open doorways drift clouds of steam, smelling of birch-bark.

The motive of their underwater stroll remains a mystery, as does their ability to survive prolonged immersion. After several hours, when the weary Noctapiolans come up on shore, they appear unable to answer any question, however reasonable. And while their doors close soundlessly upon them, the sun resumes its interrupted rising, brilliant in the vault of heaven.

26.
Utopia

The city, hexagonal, symmetrical, gleaming with cleanliness, had been endowed with every amenity of a dignified and happy existence. Deep, wide basins, connected with the course of the river, could serve in times of peace as fish thanks or swimming pools or ponds for sailboats. The city walls, uncommonly thick and concealing a maze of passages and vaults, not only presented a formidable obstacle to any assault but also provided an excellent arsenal, cool cellarage for barrels of wine and oil, spacious granaries, and highly convenient storage for vegetables and fruits. Inward from the fortified gates guarded by clock towers ran straight, paved streets, with plazas and squares at the crossings. Marble statues and fountains adorned the major squares. Sumptous stone bridges crossed the river, their arched walkways lined by charming sculptures. Every family had a pleasant home in one of the many single-story houses along the secondary streets. Every house had spacious rooms, running water, and good drains.

Along the six principal streets ran a succession of shops, workshops, factories, inns, taverns, and beerhalls; schools, barracks, and public baths. On the squares stood the guildhalls, churches, libraries, museums, courts, prisons, scaffolds, covered markets, open markets, and sports arenas. In the forum on which all six principal streets converged stood the city hall, the cathedral, the stock exchange, the university, the amphitheater, and the general meeting place of the citizens. Threaded by canals, the city abounded in parks and gardens, ponds and lakes, whose coolness refreshed the atmosphere. Everything had been thought out according to the finest models of architecture, morality, politics, and philosophy. The citizens enjoyed considerable liberty, and the officials who administered the wise laws that governed the city were elected by direct, universal suffrage.

Yet the inhabitants of the city had one, universal defect. They did not move. Like the citizens of ancient Pompeii or the people in the tale of the Sleeping Beauty, they seemed to have been immobilized by a magic wand in the strangest positions. Here, garbed in his black gown, the priest stood with his eyes fixed on the bodice of the devout parishioner kneeling before him. There, a venerable orator paused permanently in the midst of a moving address to his somnolent audience. Elsewhere an acrobat was suspended in mid-air at the height of a triple salto-mortale. A naked woman, middle-aged and flabby, posed interminably for an untalented painter. A condemned man was paralyzed, his neck an inch from the executioner's unmoving ax, under the imbecilic stare of hundreds of onlookers. A misshapen old man peered through the spyglass he had set up with which to peer at curvaceous young women in the public bath house. To the despair of his future mother, a child about to be born had changed his mind halfway. A hungry urchin sniffed forever at the odors that slipped under the door from the neighbors' kitchen. In the sordid rooms of a whorehouse several couples prolonged their momentary pleasure to infinity. At the pantomime, a pickpocket stood with his hand permanently in the mayor's assistant's purse. Beer as it was poured out hung in the air, caught between pitcher and glass…

Dissatisfied, Scamozzi tore off the sheet of paper, crumpled it up, and tossed it on the pile of unfinished sketches of the ideal city.

27.
Oldcastle

Under the cold ogived vaults of the ceilings with their fantastic ribs of stone, footsteps went on echoing for a long time. In the endless night, the curtains over the dark eye-sockets of the windows served no purpose; their vivid colors could be seen only from outside, in the rare moments when the weak, tremulous light of a candle gleamed through them. But the dwellers in the Castle were always indoors, for none of them had yet found a way out. Every door opened onto another room or another corridor.

The steps of the wooden staircases creaked hideously. Suits of armor and displays of weapons threw out strange metallic gleams. The broad stone floors were so highly polished that it was folly to venture out on them from the security of the walls. From time to time, when the echo of footsteps had died away entirely, a dreadful howling shattered the silence. Then those who dwelt in the darkness would flee in terror, knocking over halberds and suits of armor with a terrible crash, stumbling about on the stairs, bumping blindly, like deafened bats, up against pillars of ash-grey stone.

Who could tell them how they had come to be there? Those who had got used to existence in the shadowy labyrinth of the

Castle could not even remember how long they had been there, for time had lost its meaning to the point where it seemed to have ceased to pass. Newcomers, horrified at the thought of joining these generations who had dwelt seemingly forever in this nowhere, would, for a while, try hard how to find how to distinguish the living, or those they thought alive, from the ghosts. It seemed such a simple distinction, but it was difficult beyond belief.

Only when they had understood that this was not the world of the living, that they themselves were dead, could they set themselves to learn, laboriously, the ABC of the apprentice ghost: How to set footsteps echoing without taking a step. How to glide along just above the treacherous floors. And finally, when the silence grew deepest, how to produce the ghastly howling.

And so imperceptibly their spirits were calmed and soothed. They undertook the care and instruction of more recent arrivals, informing them that the night only seemed to be unending, but was interrupted at regular intervals by so-called days, during which they would go back to their places on the walls and remain immobile there in the form of portraits. Later on, they would be permitted brief interviews with dying people, even occasionally with ordinary living people.

Yet they never lost the yearning to find a way out. Just the reverse: the further their training went, the greater their determination grew. They groped through narrow passages and cellars, scrambled into attics, searched chimneys, slipped into the farthest corners of the most hermetically sealed cells, forced the rusty locks of doors, shook heavy portals that had never been opened. They held practice sessions using the apocalyptic engravings of Dürer as their model for how to wield a scythe. They thinned themselves and their garments out until at last they were able to pass through the thickest wall. Then the portraits on the castle walls, the last testimony of their passage through life, began to fade, to deteriorate, lost outline and personality, and became mere dirty scraps of canvas, while they, in groups or one by one, set off wandering through the world to fulfill what was, in the end, their destiny.

29.
Dava

So, at last, they had attained the summit! The three climbers hugged one another, speechless. Above their heads in the intensely blue sky, the same eagle was still soaring on unmoving wings, an immense eagle, loftily indifferent. They looked up at it once more, uneasily, almost with envy. Then, as if disconcerted by the haughty philosophy of the bird, they hastened to unfurl the flags of the three nations they represented.

Only when they heard the silken folds snapping in the wind of the heights did they at last look about them. They were then privileged to see the grandest view mortal eye ever beheld. The South Face, rightly considered inaccessible, was linked by a very thin, saw-toothed ridge to a second peak not shown on any map. But it was not the joy of adding a stunning geographical find to their prestigious achievement as climbers that sent a strange electric shock through them—it was the astounding shape of the newly discovered mountain. Not as high as the summit on which they stood, but even steeper, the second peak's whole upper half was shaped like a gigantic fortress with walls crowned by towers and battlements of stone. Could it be nothing but a freak of nature, a spectacular result of the inexhaustible play of chance? Hard to believe! Looked at through binoculars, the fortress presented a still more convincing display of straight lines, clean angles, smooth surfaces, orderly forms, and geometrical shapes. Everything led to the conclusion that they were seeing an immense work of human hands. But whose? Why? Above all, how? What tools could have hewn from impenetrable rock this impregnable city, heretofore completely unknown?

The minds of the three daring explorers were filled with the lure of a new adventure, more fascinating than any they could have dreamed. But their leader, though himself tempted, opposed prolonging the expedition. They had done what they set out to do. Their way back was by no means free of danger, and the descent to the nearest base camp would take several days. They were not prepared to take new and unforeseeable risks. They could return with a larger team, properly equipped and supplied.

Everything he said was perfectly logical. But as the three of them walked restlessly about the little plateau of the summit, they made a new discovery. They were not, as they had thought, the first.

The fierce winds that lash the heights had of course torn away the flags their predecessors had planted. But little by little they found unmistakable traces of at least four earlier expeditions, all thought to have been lost: two stainless steel plaques fastened to the rock, an oblong container and a hermetically sealed cylinder that contained messages and the names of explorers. Their brief disappointment gave way promptly to a burst of enthusiasm. Now it was quite clear that they must go on—their ascent was incomplete without including the fortress-peak whose silhouette hovered so temptingly south of them, not more than a day's journey away.

The decision taken, there was not a moment to lose. Night found them down on the saw-toothed ridge that served as a drawbridge to the flinty castle. Out of the question to try to set up a tent; they spent the night in sleeping bags roped down tight to the rock.

Their real test began at daybreak, as they started out across the saddleback ridge. It was so narrow that they were repeatedly forced to get astride it and drag themselves forward on their bellies. They moved very slowly, very cautiously, suspended above a gulf three thousand feet deep. Several times one or another, on the point of slipping off, was barely rescued by the other two. It was nearing nightfall when the three men, with bloody hands and clothing worn ragged, finally made it across the terrible bridge. They were utterly exhausted. It cost them a superhuman effort to climb the twenty or thirty steps that lay between them and the monumental gateway into the fortress. The doors stood open.

Seen close at hand, the fantastic citadel surpassed all imagining. The walls of living rock, brilliantly polished, were indeed a fortress one with the mountain from which it seemed to have grown. It was not, properly speaking, a building, made from blocks of stone, but rather a colossal stereotomy, a masterfully detailed three-dimensional sculpture on an immense scale. No shadow of a doubt remained: this was not the work of unaided Nature. But that certainty shed no light at all on the identity of its makers. Who were they? Who lived, or had lived, in this city? What dire necessity had forced them to create this miracle? By what strange arts had they brought it down to this solitary peak from the heights of the impossible?

Worn out, having no idea what to expect, the explorers crossed the threshold and entered the citadel. The streets were empty, lined with oddly shaped buildings, seemingly also deserted. Without their being aware of it, their weariness was dropping away, while an ever-growing curiosity drew them on. The sameness of material, the sameness of color of the structures they moved among, still very cautious, convinced them that, incredible as it might seem, the pavement, the walls, the roofs, the towers, the battlements were all parts or facets of a single stone, polished with the patience of a goldsmith. And this hallucinatory city was all the stranger for its lack of inhabitants.

Now their attention was drawn by a barely audible humming that seemed to emanate from the heart of the citadel. They hurried forward. The streets grew broader, and the buildings more imposing as they neared the center. The humming sound was louder now, with a just perceptible rhythm. The beat grew stronger. And they too were regaining strength. Soon they were almost running, paying no heed to the temples and monumental palaces that lined the street. Drawn urgently on as if irresistibly drawn by the dizzying, ever-increasing intensity of the obsessively rhythmic beat, they raced towards an unseen goal. At the end of their run, a final discovery awaited them.

On an elevated platform in the midst of a great square, hundreds of men were dancing. The sound that had drawn the explorers here was the thunderous, perfectly timed rhythm of the steps of this strange dance.

Without a second thought the newcomers dropped all they carried and joined the dancers.

Among them they recognized members of the expeditions that had climbed the peak before them, whose traces they had found the day before. They recognized other explorers who had disappeared years ago in the Alps, the Andes, the Pamir, the Himalaya, on the African savannah, in the Amazon, the outback of Australia, the icesheets of Antarctica. They recognized navigators and aviators, bold pioneers of the depths of ocean and the entrails of earth, early heroes of the epic exploration of outer space. And as the dance rose toward its climax, they saw others coming from all directions into the square.

Wholly held by the spell of the dance, they ceased to look at the others. With uplifted arms, they performed the fateful steps, feeling their limbs growing continually lighter. A painful exhilaration filled their hearts, for each one understood that the dance was plunging him into irreversible solitude. And when they saw that their arms were becoming immense wings, that feathers were covering their bodies, that their feet, turned to steely claws, were letting go of the platform, they rose up, one after another, majestic, toward the zenith, and sought to embrace, at least with their gaze, all those for whom they had carried human understanding up to these heights from which there was no return. They longed so much to tell them! But from their hooked beaks they could manage to wrench out no more than a despairing cry, which went unheard among the deep, unechoing canyons.

31.
Hattushásh

Delaporte walked towards the archeologists' camp in silence. He had gone round the walls three times and found no entrance. The fortress with its squat guard towers, incredibly situated on top of a sheer-sided mesa, remained—there was no other way to put it—impenetrable. They had no way to scale the walls, some thirty meters high and made of enormous blocks of andesite; merely getting up to them would have been impossible to a party with less skill and practice in mountain-climbing.

Delaporte shifted the coiled rope to his other shoulder. The steel rings jingled cheerfully. He looked at his swollen hands. Two fingers of the right hand hurt badly. A few paces behind him his companions on the expedition, Arik, Apurgal, and Bozkurt, came trudging along.

The savants, on the lookout for them, were gathered in front of Texier Jr's tent. Delaporte saw them from a long way off, but made no sign.

"Just as we thought," said Rosenkranz, who was as usual chewing gum.

"Of course," Kan and Balkan agreed in unison.

Ceram avoided saying anything before the little group reached them. They saw clearly enough from the weary faces of the improvised climbing party that their hope had been disappointed. They all gathered round the returned men.

"Texier discovered a city with no gates and invited us to come admire the countryside around it," Delaporte said, a dry jest without a flicker of emotion.

"In short," Bozkurt confirmed, "we accomplished nothing."

"Nothing at all?"

"Nothing," Arik said bitterly.

They were all silent. Texier felt obliged to justify himself—"I'm not to blame for the fact that there's no way in. And that fact, you must realize, makes my discovery still more sensational. To come across something like this, totally unexpected—a perfectly preserved city maybe three thousand years old!"

"Fine, but what can we do with it?"

A long discussion ensued. Forrer proposed digging a tunnel into the rocky mesa, which would bring them up inside the city walls. Laroche argued strenuously against this, insisting that dynamiting a section of the wall would be more practicable. Messerschmidt suggested that they arrange for bombardment from the air, recommending the use of helicopters. Moortgat categorically opposed it— "I'll die before I agree to that! To have the incredible luck of finding a city that's remained undestroyed for three millennia and then destroy it—*we* destroy it—we archeologists? As if we can't exist anywhere but amidst ruins?"

Delaporte thought it time to intervene. "Moortgat's right," he said. "It might annoy the inhabitants."

"Inhabitants?" shouted Hogarth.

"The city is inhabited," Bozkurt confirmed.

"While we were climbing up to it, we heard them talking," said Akurgal. "Loud, penetrating voices."

"And you waited till now to tell us?" growled Hrozny, who had been struggling for weeks to deduce the builders' language from the layout of the walls. "What were they saying?"

"I could only be sure of two words, which they kept saying: *múrsilis* and *hántilis*."

Hrozny stood with his mouth open. "Just as I thought," he stammered. "Listen—we can try to communicate with them!"

All the archeologists hurried to the mesa, Texier leading the way with agility surprising in a man of his age. Porada and Koschakev followed close on his heels, and after them the rest of expedition, the exhausted men who had just returned to camp trailing along last. They were all talking at the same time, filled with a sudden, suspect enthusiasm.

"We can always try the Trojan Horse trick," Rosenkranz said.

"Communication!" shouted Hrozny, terribly excited; he had managed, despite the haste of their departure, to bring a megaphone.

"*Múrsilis*," Delaporte kept muttering.

"Silence," Texier commanded, as they approached the foot of the mesa.

When the chatter had ceased, Hrozny lifted the megaphone to his lips and bellowed into it with all his strength: "*Sullat, sullatár, sullami salatiwár!*"

A chorus of voices instantly responded from within the walls: "*Labárna hastdya, tabdrna asharpdia!*"

"What the devil's all that about?" Ceram fumed. Texier motioned him to keep silent. Hrozny shrugged his shoulders, disconcerted, to signify that he had understood nothing.

"*Mitánni! Mitánni!*" he roared desperately into the megaphone in a last, futile effort to find a common language.

There was no reply.

The grey walls of the fortress gave a menacing air to the minutes of absolute silence. Then all at once, around both ends of the mesa, the Hittite warriors appeared with drawn bows and bronze axes, in swift war-chariots drawn by small horses. The deafening creak of high wooden wheels drowned out the hoof-beats and the savage war-cries of the long-haired attackers. The archeologists were caught in a fatal ambush, without hope of resistance.

The chariots halted abruptly.

"*Hattilí supiluliúma,*" a warrior on the right wing called out, as if opening negotiations.

"Don't answer!" Moortgat shouted to Hrozny. "He's trying to challenge us to fight!"

"*Assúwa samúha tawanánna,*" the warrior insisted.

"*Karkemísh gasgás datsdssa,*" added a man from the left wing.

From inside the fortress the invisible chorus was heard—
"Ziúla, zálpa huwarúwas! Ziúla, zálpa huwarúwas!"

The warriors grew more threatening—*"Hattushil gurgúm kumúhu, telipínu putuhepa!"*—*"Hánis kánes pihassássis, hátti hálys muwatállis!"*—*"Arnuwándas kizzuwátna, pentipsáni purushánda, pámba pála tapassánda!"*

The first to die was Hrozny, his heart unable to support the lexical avalanche. The Hittites loosed their arrows, hurled their axes with deadly aim. Many of the savants, mortally wounded, fell. The chief of the warriors lifted his arm to halt the attack.

"Vous avez voulu voir Hattushásh," he called out in schoolbook French. "Hé bien, vous allez être exaucés!" (You wanted to see Hattushash? Well, you'll get what you wanted!)

Warriors tied up the few survivors lying mute on the ground, and dumped the dead into the war-chariots. Delaporte was howling horribly in his death agony, and they ran a spear through him. At that moment, with a sinister grating noise, a door swung open among the rocks at the foot of the mesa. Within moments the Hittites, with their horses, chariots, and prisoners, had vanished into the black opening. The door closed, becoming solid rock again. And within a few more minutes all trace of the incident was gone, while the walls of the fortress noiselessly crumbled away, as if in a dream.

Since that time no one has seen the honorable savants, members of the archeological expedition mounted by Texier Jr. Only the mute testimony of deserted camp remained for a time to tell the world of its tragic close. Then the wind and the rain

and the curiosity of the natives of the region shredded away
one tent after another into many-colored dust.

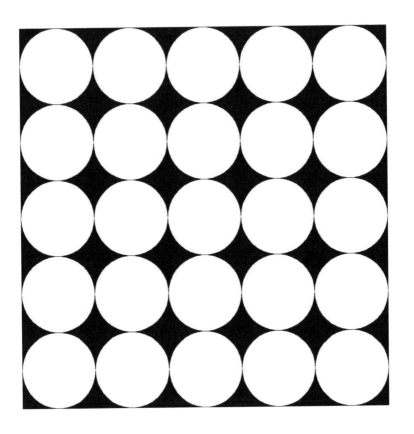

32.
Selenia

They were looking for a site on which to found the first city on the Moon. The problems presented by a rough, broken terrain were greatly increased by the litter previous visitors had scattered over the whole surface of Earth's only natural satellite. The uninformed might well assume that this refuse consisted of tin cans, broken bottles, waste paper, cigarette butts and packets and such rubbish, orange rinds, nutshells, streetcar tickets, subway tickets, spaceship tickets; but that disgusting detritus of sloth is to be found only on Earth, in the last places one wants to find it—on mountaintops and glacial cirques, by the banks of crystalline alpine rivers, beside springs, in woods, among flowers of glade and meadow, on the golden sea-beaches. The Moon had accumulated no such material litter, but it had suffered from pollution of a very different nature, subtler, yet incomparably more damaging.

Not only those who had set foot in person on this alluring celestial body, from Cyrano de Bergerac and Baron Munchhausen to the astronauts of twentieth-century lunar missions, but also those who had described it, sung about it, dreamed of it, or merely looked at it, along with all the lunatics of the ages, and all the people who had prayed to it or worshipped it and woven enchanting myths about its nightly appearances—every last one had contributed, unknowingly, to this irreversible process.

To be sure, a person staying only briefly in the contaminated areas might go almost unaffected, but a longer visit, and certainly a prolonged stay, let alone the permanent settlement implied in the then popular project of establishing an urban grid, proved to be totally impracticable. Investigations revealed an advanced state of spiritual pollution, a slow, progressive degradation dating from the earliest days of civilization on Earth and still continuing unabated. No law had ever protected the Moon from this imponderable assault, the effects of which were still not fully understood.

It was clear that, at least on the face of the Moon visible from Earth, it would be very difficult to find a protected area, a "natural preserve." It had been completely taken over by phantoms, specters, meditations, emotions, fragments of ideas, and exclamation points. People staying there found it real torture to try to follow the course of their thoughts through the labyrinth created by the emanations of other minds, some of which had spent millennia wandering about in a vacuum.

Small wonder, then, that they had trouble finding a site for the first city, which was to have borne the resounding name of Selenia. The expedition soon resolved to extend their explorations to the far side of the Moon. From there, maintaining contact with Earth would certainly be more difficult for the future inhabitants of the projected settlement; but there was some justification for the hope of finding on the outer side a purer psychic ambience. The arguments for it appeared perfectly sound.

Yet, having made the extremely circuitous and tremendously dangerous journey to the far side, they were stupefied to find that the situation was no better—if anything, worse. The aggressive influx of images, the unsettling onslaught of ideas from other minds was even more ferocious and unrelenting. Most disturbing of all was the strangeness of these ideas, the fact that it was impossible to explain them in any way, because they could neither describe them exactly nor comprehend their nature at all.

They gradually began to be able to distinguish certain general characteristics: for example, mystical and poetical thoughts were extremely rare here, almost non-existent, whereas scientific arguments, pragmatic considerations, and calls to action abounded. It would seem that the Moon acted like blotting paper or a filter—a selective filter, permitting only certain emanations (the most recent ones, as if its permeability to this curious osmosis was increasing with time on a logarithmic curve) to pass from the near side to the far side, while blocking out all the others. Yet, logically, such osmosis should have resulted in a lower concentration of contemporary thoughts, a higher concentration of ancient thoughts, on the face visible from Earth, and such was not the case.

They tried in vain to solve the enigma. Many thoughts, the presence of which could be established only at a vast expense of nervous energy, remained exasperatingly inaccessible, their meaning beyond comprehension. This inaccessibility, indeed, at last gave rise to a hypothesis which, though unproven, won general support: to wit, that while the contamination of the lunar face visible from Earth was due to the Moon's presence in terrestrial, human minds, the pollution of the far side proceeded from extraterrestrial civilizations sufficiently advanced to have been able to observe the existence of Earth's satellite. That influence would surely be far less pervasive on the face of the Moon permanently turned to the Earth.

Whatever the explanation, the contamination of both faces of the Moon was an unquestionable fact. Until some remedy could be found, the earthlings would have to renounce their colonization project, which as it stood at that time seemed to run contrary to the plans and calculations of other inhabited worlds, and content themselves with brief visits. Selenia must remain, or so it seemed, a city never founded. In reality, it covered the whole surface of the Moon, and had been populated since the most remote antiquity.

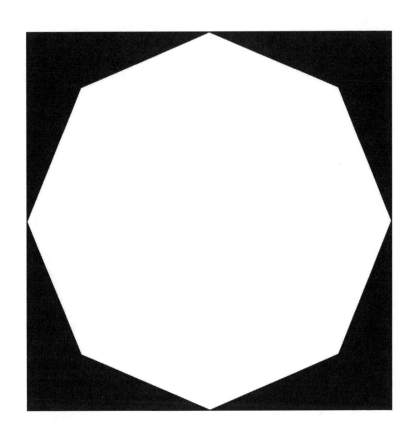

33.
Antar

The city was built of blocks of ice, the hard, translucent ice of Antarctica, on which it stood and from which it took its name. We must not be misled by the fact that the *Petit Larousse* (1968 edition, page 1,123, column three) limited its article on Antar or Antara to "Sixth-century Arabic warrior-poet, hero of the epic *Romance of Antar*," with no reference at all to the world's southernmost city. The similarity of the names is purely coincidental. The failure of the prestigious encyclopedia, even in more recent editions, to mention the city, is unjustifiable, but easily explained: Antar was fated by the supreme brevity of its existence to take no lasting place in history. What I write here is a mere attempt at the posthumous correction of an injustice. (Less prejudiced encyclopedias also omit mention of the obscure Arabic warrior-poet.)

The Antarians took legitimate pride in the fact that the sun had never risen above the horizon during the entire period of the existence of their settlement. Furthermore, it should be said that, far from being boastful as they might well have been, these good people were, though uncommunicative, notably modest. Their undeniably icy character, their formal conduct, their distant, meditative bearing, brought upon them more than one accusation of pride and misanthropy, but such judgments, as will be seen from what follows, were hasty and unfair.

The fact is unquestionable that, except for the austral aurora, starlight, and Zodiacal light, the city lived in darkness, in a night without end—and, according to some, without beginning.

Thus it is easy to understand how pleasing to the municipal administration was the striking and inexplicable luminosity of the citizens. Since their entire bodies glowed with a strong, diffuse, bluish light, there was no need to provide lighting in the streets or houses. Unfortunately no one ever saw them, since for unknown reasons outsiders were strictly banned from the city, but the sight must have been magical: a coming and going of phosphorescent bodies in the streets and within half-transparent housewalls, worthy of the brush of the greatest poets of light, from Rembrandt to de Chirico.

Undoubtedly, obeying its own slow rhythm, the Antarian way of life would have received the consecration of history and geography, adding a new name to the maps and manuals, new passages to the historical records, new articles to encyclopedias. But an adverse destiny soon reduced such possibilities to zero. The premature ending of all the hopes of the city was brought about, paradoxically, by its growing fame, the self-imposed mystery of its isolation, the legend that began to be woven about its name.

Joe had no job or position in the usual sense of the word. All day long, and especially all night long, for he had a strong, unspoken preference for performing at night, he did nothing but perfect the art of striking the well-stretched drumhead of a tomtom with his palms, his fingers, his fist, his wrists and elbows, his forehead, even his chin. It bothered him not at all that people around him looked after the insignificant details of his daily life, just as he cared not at all whether they liked his performance or not. Joe drummed simply because it was impossible for him not to. Exactly how he managed the risky business of getting into Antar no one knows—he, of all people, interested in nothing but his drum, unable to keep anything in his head beyond pounding rhythmically on a drumhead. There is no way to know how he heard about the city or by what miracles he reached it. The only perfectly certain fact is that, once there, he went on diligently drumming.

The consequences were startling: before the authorities were alerted and might have expelled the intruder, it was too late to do anything. In fact the chain reaction effect was barely notice-able at first, and that sealed the city's fate. When the Antar-ians heard Joe drumming, and we have to admit that he was a terrific drummer, they began moving a little faster. That was all. Yet this minuscule acceleration brought about its inexorable result. Nobody paid any attention to the black man who, apparently oblivious to anything going on around him, sent his fiery rhythms pounding on the air. But people kept moving always a little bit faster, as if under a spell; and as the acceleration increased, the luminosity of their bodies intensified, taking on a yellowish-red hue. Passersby came to look like walking torches. And then, to general consternation, the city began to melt—so rapidly that soon no trace of it remained. Most Antarians, left out in the open with the ice melting under their feet, went into exile. And as if the fulminating combustion had burnt them out, they lost their luminosity.

It is said that when asked, later on, what had induced him to settle in the city nearest the South Pole, Joe answered simply, "Somebody told me those people had never heard a tomtom." None the less, one of his most competent biographers is inclined to believe that what drew him irresistibly to Antar was the dream of a night that would never end.

34.
Atlantis

The triumphal reception had been prepared down to the last detail, and the waiting crowd was expecting the Saviors to appear at any moment. Everybody knew the mysterious visitors would be instantly recognizable, though who they were and what they looked like no one knew; and as to whence they came and their means of transportation, the sacred prophetic books of the Atlanteans spoke, incomprehensibly, only of the future.

As zero hour approached, every living soul in the great city had joined the crowd on the broad central agora. The shadow of the gnomon moved slowly across the white surface of an immense sundial. Everyone watched in silence, with intense emotion, as it neared the red stripe that would signal the final act of the drama. The faith of the people in the sacred prophecy was unwavering, but all were aware of a strange presentiment, a vague fear, augmented by the mystical awe of the solemn moment.

The rest of the city stood empty; every street and square but the central one had fallen still, even before the establishment of the millennial reign of silence. Fortifications cut from the lava of extinct volcanoes circled this citadel of luxury and splendor, giving it a convincing look of invincibility, but no protection from a telluric attack. The magnificent palaces full of unimaginable treasures were about to be hidden forever from covetous eyes.

A shadow, like an evil omen, fell across the crimson stripe in the marble of the sundial, and at that very moment the city was rocked to its foundations by a shock of colossal power. The ground shook, the earth broke open like a crust of bread. And shining Atlantis began to sink majestically into the depths, taking with it the destiny of an entire empire.

Despite the general panic, despite their outlandish clothing, the visitors were recognized at once.

Members of a spatio-temporal expedition motivated by scientific and (it may as well be added) journalistic curiosity, they had succeeded in arriving in time to witness the destruction of Atlantis, an event that their information ascribed to geological accident. But their formidable time machine was now malfunctioning. There was no chance that a second expedition could arrive in time to rescue them from the disaster of the first. Abandoned among the heroic barbarians of protohistory, exposed to the dreadful consequences of the cataclysm, separated perhaps forever from their contemporaries, their situation did not strike them as promising.

None the less they found the strength to accept the destiny thrust upon them, that of saviors who must use all their intelligence and knowledge to further the ultimate unfolding of a history which, after all, though in general terms, they knew.

"Down to the harbor!" they commanded, and the Atlanteans followed them without a murmur. "Take provisions only, as much as possible! Our salvation is the sea!"

So they sailed away from the continent over whose ruin the Atlantic Ocean would roll. Many ships sank under the implacable battering of the waves; for every life saved, dozens were lost. The survivors dispersed throughout the world and, following the counsel of the sanctified Saviors, founded civilizations that were for a long time believed to be the earliest.

There were many attempts to find those first explorers of the Past. But those who survived the shipwrecks of the great exodus, elevated into God-Kings, honored as bringers of enlightenment, were indisposed to renounce their calling. Not one of them has ever returned to our era. We still cannot answer the question of whether the time machine's failure was caused by the geological catastrophe or by a fault in the propulsion system. Nor can we entirely dismiss the possibility that the failure was deliberately induced by the time-travelers themselves.

35.
Quanta Ka

Almost every observatory in the Northern hemisphere reported the phenomenon: the appearance, in the direction of the North Star, of a powerful source of emissions different from any known type of radiation. Though without luminosity, the signal registered on photographic film; though not a radio wave, any radio receiver could produce it as sound; not electromagnetic, yet it showed up on the whole length of the spectrum, in every frequency. And most surprising of all, most disconcerting to physicists, was the fact that in all probability its velocity exceeded that of light.

Astrophysicists soon determined that this new form of radiation was not homogeneous and not emitted steadily, but displayed a series of variations that registered on every wavelength of the electromagnetic spectrum: a fixed modulation, repeated rhythmically, always identical. These variations, occurring in about a millionth of a second, were called by the initial letter of the discoverer's last name—K quanta (in Europe, quanta Ka).

After several weeks the emission ceased as suddenly as it had begun. The K quantum continued to preoccupy learned minds all over the world for a considerable time, but as all investigation continued fruitless, the passion aroused in the scientific community faded little by little and died out. Only a fanatic here and there went on investigating the K phenomenon, mostly in secret, to avoid becoming a laughing-stock. And even they admitted failure at last.

But after some time a young man, captivated by the idea that the mysterious quanta might be a signal sent out into the cosmos by another civilization, dedicated himself to deciphering the hypothetical communication, and shut himself up in his laboratory for more than twenty years. There with the passion of a true pioneer he brought together every document related to the object of his investigation. He set up an astronomical observatory equipped with a powerful radiotelescope and high-quality instruments and apparatus that allowed him to keep under close and constant observation the section of the heavens in which, nearly a half century before, the source had been located. His investigations were so far successful as to convince him that he was on the right track; he had incontrovertible evidence that as he had thought all along, he was dealing with a message. But he could not find the key to it, he was no further in deciphering it than when he began. He was sure that his search was blocked because all he had was secondary evidence, recordings made with inadequate equipment, nonspecific, foreign to the nature of the emission, which could communicate only a shadow of the actual message. He could succeed only if the emission were repeated. So he concentrated wholly on making sure that in that eventuality he would be in immediate contact with the K quanta, able to investigate them as they occurred. He saw his advantage over the original discoverers as not only the possession of more advanced instruments, but also the radically different orientation of his research, based on his conviction that he was dealing with a signal, a possibility his predecessors had discounted.

He continued hopeful. He was no longer a boy, but was still full of energy and felt that he had enough years yet to live that he could allow himself hope. In any case, there was nothing else for him to do, other than abandon the search, which never occurred to him. Daily he checked his equipment and modified the settings; nightly he studied the North Star, certain that the message would be repeated. And indeed the miracle occurred! From the moment he recognized the signal he abandoned everything else, even sleep, spending his nights and days listening to it.

He was in his laboratory surrounded by the entire complex of instruments and apparatus that he had conceived, planned, and built with such tenacity. His attention at maximum intensity, his nerves barely under control, he maintained an unbroken observation of the energy fluctuation whose hidden significance he had sought in vain, until this moment. All at once he felt as if struck by lightning. The last image in his brain was of the huge electronic chronometer, which he had mounted directly in fro-nt of his eyes.

He found himself in an unknown city, seeming to drift among buildings of a completely unfamiliar kind. The sky was violet and the light very intense, though there was no sun to be seen. He felt that he was being watched, but saw no one; the walls of the buildings were opaque. Perhaps, he thought, they were impenetrable to his gaze and allowed light to pass through them only in one direction. Or else what he was feeling was the steady gaze of the surrounding buildings themselves, not mere constructions but actual living beings, enormously large.... Was he in fact in a city? Or in a forest, or a herd, or a crowd? He drifted as if in a dream, effortlessly, carried along by a force from which he could not escape but which seemed, in a way, to oblige his curiosity as a sight-seer.

He was not hungry, thirsty, or sleepy, although as well as he could estimate the journey went on for a long time, possibly for years. The limitless city he was visiting, if it was a city, was inhabited, and he would have liked to know the inhabitants. It seemed discourteous and unjust to him that they should keep him in this situation of inferiority, exposed to the gaze of all, while he could see nobody.

As if his wish had been overheard, he saw a creature coming to meet him, drifting along in the same gliding flight. He ceased to pay attention to any of the seeming buildings, gazing at it, fascinated. It had no resemblance at all to a human being, and he could not tell if it was male or female (or asexual or hermaphrodite), yet he felt the kind of attraction to it that an Italian might feel for a magnificent, blue-eyed, Swedish blonde. The middle-aged man felt the vigor of his youth revive. The two circled about each other in an aerial dance that built up in him an amazing erotic tension, an experience of such intensity as to be almost unbearable, even as his heart burned with yearning to prolong it infinitely, to gain eternity, to be interfused with the whole Universe.

When he came back to himself in the laboratory facing the chronometer, it was, unbelievably, in the same fraction of a second. And at once he realized that he had deciphered— more than that, had lived—a fragment of the message he had spent so many years trying to understand. The city of his momentary vision (which in his memoirs he would call Quanta Ka) belonged to another world and was evidently inhabited by creatures such as the one he had known. He was painfully shaken by the memory. Never could he accept the idea (though he could not entirely drive it away) that in all probability they would never meet again. The knowledge that they might never have met at all, that it had all been due to mere chance, had no effect on his passionate longing.

His scientific curiosity had vanished and now seemed empty and absurd. He had lost all interest in the message itself. The goal of his life henceforth was to meet once more with the creature that had been so cruelly snatched from him. And yet, in all truth, fate had treated him with considerable generosity; he had been granted the terrible and marvelous moment. A second chance at it was too much to ask.

Translator Biography

Ursula Kroeber Le Guin was born in 1929 in Berkeley, and lives in Portland. As of 2012, she has published twenty-one novels, eleven volumes of short stories, four collections of essays, twelve books for children, six volumes of poetry and four of translation, and has received many honors and awards. Previous translations from Spanish include the *Selected Poems* of Gabriela Mistral and *Kalpa Imperial* by Angelica Gorodischer.

Author Biography

Born on April 9, 1941, in Bucharest, Romania, Gheorghe Săsărman spent his childhood and attended high-school in Cluj, Transylvania's capital-city. He studied architecture in Bucharest and after graduation was employed as a journalist, authoring articles on architecture and popular science. In 1978 he received his PhD in the theory of architecture. Politically constrained to abandon his activity as a media writer, he left Ceaușescu's Romania in 1983 and settled in Munich, Germany, where he worked as a computer programmer and analyst. He is married, has a daughter (35) and a son (30) and has recently become a grandfather.

After the fall of the communist regime (1989) he resumed his activity as a journalist, contributing to Romanian newspapers and magazines and to various publications of the Romanian diaspora texts later collected in the volume *Between Parallel Mirrors* (2009). Between 2006 and 2010, in Munich, he edited the review *The Apposition*, a *sui-generis* almanach written by Romanian-born men of culture living abroad. He is a member of the Professional Journalists' Union and of the Romanian Writers' Union.

Săsărman made his debut as a writer in 1962, when he won the first prize at an SF short-story contest organized for seven East-European countries. His first book, *The Oracle* (1969) grouped texts previously published in periodicals. S*quaring the Circle* (1975) clashed with the communist censorship, which cut out one quarter of its contents; it has since been published in

France (1994) and Spain (2010). A story in the volume *Chimera* (1979), "Algernon's Escape"—whose title paraphrases that of Daniel Keyes's famous novel—brought the author the Europa Award at the Eurocon V Convention (1980). The novel *2000* (1982) was published in German in Munich as *Die Enklaven der Zeit* (1986). After 1989, he resumed publishing fiction in his native country: the novels *The Hemlock Cup* (1994), *South vs. North* (2001), *The Unparallelled Adventures of Anton Retegan and of His Secret Police File* (2011), as well as the short-story collection *Visions* (2007). His play *Deus ex Machina* was staged in Munich (2005) and Bucharest (2006-2009). Săsărman has published short stories and novellas in magazines, anthologies and collective volumes in Romania, Germany, France, Italy, Spain, Poland, Hungary, and Japan. In 2012, he was awarded the "Ion Hobana" Opera Omnia Prize by the Bucharest branch of the Writers' Union and the Romanian Association for Science Fiction and Fantasy.